I0567580

Some Tales In Verse by Richard Doddriage Blackmore

Richard Doddridge Blackmore was born on 7 June 1825 at Longworth in Berkshire (now part of Oxfordshire), where his father, John Blackmore, was Curate-in-charge of the parish. His mother died a few months after his birth, the victim of an outbreak of typhus. With this loss the family moved to Bushey, Hertfordshire, then on to their native Devon. His elder brother Richard (by a year), however, was taken by his aunt to live near Oxford. His father married again in 1831, whereupon Richard returned to live with them. With much of his childhood spent in the lush and pastoral "Doone Country" of Exmoor, and along the Badgworthy Water, Blackmore came to love the very countryside he immortalised in Lorna Doone. In November 1853 he married his wife Lucy. And the following year, 1854, his literary career began with a collection of Poems and for the next 15 years he would write in the winters and garden in the summers. In 1860 with inherited money he built a house in Teddington just outside of London and established a market garden for the cultivation of fruit. He loved horticulture but having little business experience could never really exploit it. However with the publication of Lorna Doone in 1869 he was catapulted to fame. And although he continued to write extensively nothing caught the public imagination quite like Lorna Doone. In the stories collected here much of that countryside character comes through to counterpoint the strong characters he creates. RD Blackmore died at Teddington on 20 January 1900 after a long and painful illness, and was buried next to his wife in Teddington cemetery. Here we publish 'Some Tales In Verse' which show yet another side of this great author's talents.

Index Of Contents

Fringilla loquitur

"What means your finch?"

"Being well aware that he cannot sing like a Nightingale,
He flits about from tree to tree, and twitters a little tale."

Albeit he is an ancient bird, who tried his pipe in better days, and then was scared by random shots, he is fain to lift the migrant wing once more towards the humble perch, among the trees he loves. All gardeners own that he does no harm, unless he flits into a thicket of young buds, or a very choice ladies' seed-bed. And he hopes that he is now too wise to commit such indiscretions.

Perhaps it would have been wiser still to have shut up his little mandible, or employed it only upon grub. But the long gnaw of last winter's frost, which set mankind a-shivering, even in their most downy nest, has made them kindly to the race that has no roof for shelter and no hearth for warmth.

Anyhow, this little finch can do no harm, if he does no good; and if he pleases nobody, he will not be surprised, because he has never satisfied himself.

May-day, 1895.

TO MY PEN

I
Thou feeble implement of mind,
Wherewith she strove to scrawl her name;
But, like a mitcher, left behind
No signature, no stroke, no claim,
No hint that she hath pined

Shall ever come a stronger time,
When thou shalt be a tool of skill,
And steadfast purpose, to fulfil
A higher task than rhyme?

II
Thou puny instrument of soul,
Wherewith she labours to impart
Her efforts at some arduous goal;
But fails to bring thy coarser art
Beneath a fine control

Shall ever come a fairer day,
When thou shalt be a buoyant plume,
To soar, where clearer suns illume,
And fresher breezes play?

III
Thou weak interpreter of heart,
So impotent to tell the tale
Of love's delight, of envy's smart,
Of passion, and ambition's bale,
Of pride that dwells apart

Shall I, in length of time, attain
(By walking in the human ways,

With love of Him, who made and sways)
To ply thee, less in vain?

If so, thou shalt be more to me
Than sword, or sceptre, flag, or crown;
With mind, and soul, and heart in thee,
Despising gold, and sham renown;

But truthful, kind, and free
Then come; though now a pithless quill,
Uncouth, unfledged, indefinite,
In time, thou shalt be taught to write,
By patience, and good-will.

LITA OF THE NILE

A TALE IN THREE PARTS

PART I

I
"King, and Father, gift and giver,
God revealed in form of river,
Issuing perfect, and sublime,
From the fountain-head of time;

"Whom eternal mystery shroudeth,
Unapproached, untracked, unknown;
Whom the Lord of heaven encloudeth
With the curtains of His throne;

"From the throne of heaven descending,
Glory, power, and goodness blending,
Grant us, ere the daylight dies,
Token of thy rapid rise,"

II
Ha, it cometh! Furrowing, flashing,
Red blood rushing o'er brown breast;
Peaks, and ridges, and domes, dashing
Foam on foam, and crest on crest!

'Tis the signal Thebes hath waited,
Libyan Thebes, the hundred-gated:
Rouse, and robe thee, River-priest
For thy dedication feast!

Follows him the loveliest maiden,
Afric's thousand hills can show;
White apparel'd, flower-laden,
With the lotus on her brow.

III
Votive maid, who hath espousal
Of the river's high carousal;
Twenty cubits if he rise,
This shall be his bridal prize.

Calm, and meek of face and carriage,
Deigning scarce a quicker breath,
Comes she to the funeral marriage,
The betrothal of black death.

Rosy hands, and hennaed fingers,
Nails whereon the onyx lingers,
Clasped, as at a lover's tale,
In the bosom's marble vale.

IV
Silvery scarf, her waist enwreathing,
Wafts a soft Sabaean balm;
Like a cloud of incense, breathing
Round the column of a palm:

Snood of lilies interweaveth
(Giving less than it receiveth)
Beauty of her clustered brow,
Calmly bent upon us now.

Through her dark hair, spread before
See the western glory wane,
As in groves of dim Cytorus,
Or the bowers of Taprobane!

V
See, the large eyes, lit by heaven,
Brighter than the Sisters Seven,
(Like a star the storm hath cowed)
Sink their flash in sorrow's cloud.

There the crystal tear refraineth,
And the founts of grief are dry;
"Father, Mother, none remaineth;

All are dead; and why not I?"

Yet, by God's will, heavenly beauty
Owes to Heaven alone its duty;
Off ye priests, who dare adjudge
Bride, like this, to slime and sludge!

VI
When they tread the river's margent,
All their mitred heads are bowed
What hath browned the ripples argent,
Like the plume of thunder-cloud?

Where yestreen the water slumbered,
With a sickly crust encumbered,
Leapeth now a roaring flood,
Wild as war, and red as blood.

Every billow hurries quicker,
Every surge runs up the strand;
While the brindled eddies flicker,
Scourged as with a levin brand.

VII
Every bulrush, parched and welted,
Lifts his long joints yellow-belted;
Every lotus, faint and sick,
Hangs her fragrant tongue to lick.

Countless creatures, lone unthought of,
Swarm from every hole and nook;
What is man, that he make nought of
Other entries in God's book?

Scorpions, rats, and lizards flabby,
Centipedes, and hydras scabby,
Asp, and slug, and toad, whose gem
Outlasts human diadem.

VIII
Therefore hath the priest-procession
Causeway clean of sandal-wood;
That no foul thing make transgression
On the votive maiden's blood.

Pure of blood and soul, she standeth
Where the marble gauge demandeth,

Marble pillar, with black style,
Record of the rising Nile,

White-robed priests around her kneeling,
Ibis-banner floating high,
Conchs, and drums, and sistrals pealing,
And Sesostris standing nigh.

IX
He, whose kingdom-city stretches
Further than our eyesight fetches;
Every street it wanders down
Larger than a regal town;

Built, when each man was a giant,
When the rocks were mason's stones,
When the oaks were osiers pliant,
And the mountains scarcely thrones;

City, whose Titanic portals
Scorn the puny modern mortals,
In thy desert winding-sheet,
Sacred from our insect feet.

X
Thebes No-Amon, hundred-gated,
Every gate could then unfold
Cavalry ten thousand, plated,
Man and horse, in solid gold.

Glancing back through serried ranges,
Vivid as his own phalanges,
Every captain might espy
Equal host in sculpture vie;

Down Piromid vista gazing,
Ten miles back from every gate,
He can see that temple blazing,
Which the world shall never mate.

XI
But the Nile-flood, when it swelleth,
Recks not man, nor where he dwelleth;
And e'en while Sesostris reigns
Scarce five cubits man attains.

Lo, the darkening river quaileth,

Like a swamp by giant trod,
And the broad commotion waileth,
Stricken with the hand of God I

When the rushing deluge raging
Flung its flanks, and shook the staging,
Priesthood, cowering from the brim,
Chanted thus its faltering hymn.

XII
"Ocean sire, the earth enclasping,
Like a babe upon thy knee,
In thy cosmic cycle grasping
All that hath been, or shall be;

"Thou, that art around and over
All we labour to discover;
Thou, to whom our world no more
Than a shell is on thy shore;

"God, that wast Supreme, or ever
Orus, or Osiris, saw;
God, with whom is no endeavour,
But thy will eternal law:

XIII
"We, who keep thy feasts and fastings,
We, who live on thy off-castings,
Here in low obeisance crave
Rich abundance of thy wave.

"Seven years now, for some transgression,
Some neglect, or outrage vile,
Vainly hath our poor procession
Offered life, and soul to Nile.

"Seven years now of promise fickle,
Niggard ooze, and paltry trickle,
Freshet sprinkling scanty dole,
Where the roaring flood should roll.

XIV
"Therefore are thy children dwindled,
Therefore is thine altar bare;
Wheat, and rye, and millet spindled,
And the fruits of earth despair.

"Men with haggard bellies languish,
Bridal beds are strewn with anguish,
Mothers sell their babes for bread,
Half the holy kine are dead.

"Is thy wrath at last relaxing?
Art thou merciful, once more?
Yea, behold the torrent waxing!
Yea, behold the flooded shore!

XV
"Nile, that now with life-blood tidest,
And in gorgeous cold subsidest,
Richer than our victor tread
Stirred in far Hydaspes' bed;

"When thy swelling crest o'er-waveth
Yonder twenty cubit mark,
And thy tongue of white foam laveth
Borders of the desert dark,

"This, the fairest Theban maiden,
Shall be thine, with jewels laden;
Lift thy furrowed brow, and see
Lita, dedicate to thee!"

XVI
Thus he spake, and lowly stooping
O'er the Calasiris hem,
Took the holy water, scooping
With a bowl of lucid gem;

Chanting from the Bybline psalter
Touched he then her forehead altar;
Sleeking back the trickled jet,
There the marriage-seal he set.

"None of mortals dare pursue thee,
None come near thy hallowed side:
Nile's thou art, and he shall woo thee,
Nile, who swalloweth his bride."

XVII
With despair's mute self-reliance,
She accepted death's affiance;
She, who hath no home or rest,
Shrank not from the river's breast.

Haply there she shall discover
Father, lost in wilds unknown,
Mother slain, and youthful lover,
Seen as yet in dreams alone.

Ha! sweet maid, what sudden vision
Hath dispelled thy cold derision?
What new picture hast thou seen,
Of a world that might have been?

XVIII
From Mount Seir, Duke Iram roveth,
Three renewals of the moon:
To see Egypt him behoveth,
Ere his life be past its noon.

Soul, and mind, at first fell under
Flat discomfiture of wonder,
With the Nile before him spread,
Temple-crowned, and tempest-fed!

Yet a nobler creed he owneth,
Than to worship things of space:
One true God his heart enthroneth
Heart that throbs with Esau's race.

XIX
Thus he stood, with calm eyes scorning
Idols, priests, and their adorning;
Seeing, e'en in nature's show,
Him alone, who made it so.

"God of Abraham, our Father,
Earth, and heaven, and all we see,
Are but gifts of thine, to gather
Us, thy children, back to Thee.

"All the grandeur spread before us,
All the miracles shed o'er us,
Echoes of the voice above,
Tokens of a Father's love."

XX
While of heaven his heart indited,
And his dark eyes swept the crowd,
Sudden on the maid they lighted,

Mild and haughty, meek and proud.

Rapid as the flash of sabre,
Strong as giant's toss of caber,
Sure as victor's grasp of goal,
Came the love-stroke through his soul

Gently she, her eyes recalling,
Felt that Heaven had touched their flight,
Peeped again, through lashes falling,
Blushed, and shrank, and shunned the light

XXI
Ah, what booteth sweet illusion,
Fluttering glance, and soft suffusion,
Bliss unknown, but felt in sighs,
Breast, that shrinks at its own rise?

She, who is the Nile's devoted,
Courted with a watery smile;
Her betrothal duly noted
By the bridesmaid Crocodile!

So she bowed her forehead lowly,
Tightened her tiara holy;
And, with every sigh suppressed,
Clasped her hands on passion's breast.

PART II

I
Twice the moon hath waxed and wasted,
Lavish of her dew-bright horn;
And the wheeling sun hath hasted
Fifty days, towards Capricorn.

Thebes, and all the Misric nation,
Float upon the inundation;
Each man shouts and laughs, before
Landing at his own house door.

There the good wife doth return it,
Grumbling, as she shows the dish,
Chervil, basil, chives, and burnet
Feed, instead of seasoning, fish.

II
Palm trees, grouped upon the highland,
Here and there make pleasant island;
On the bark some wag hath wrote
"Who would fly, when he can float?"

Udder'd cows are standing, pensive,
Not belonging to that ilk;
How shall horn, or tail defensive,
Keep the water from their milk?

Lo, the black swan, paddling slowly,
Pintail ducks, and sheldrakes holy,
Nile-goose flaked, and herons gray,
Silver-voiced at fall of day!

III
Flood hath swallowed dikes and hedges,
Lately by Sesostris planned;
Till, like ropes, its matted edges
Quiver on the desert sand.

Then each farmer, brisk and mellow,
Graspeth by the hand his fellow;
And, as one gone labour-proof,
Shakes his head at the drowned shadoof

Soon the Nuphar comes, beguiling
Sedgy spears, and swords around,
Like that cradled infant smiling,
Whom, the royal maiden found.

IV
But the time of times foe wonder,
Is when ruddy sun goes under;
And the dusk throws, half afraid,
Silver shuttles of long shade.

Opens then a scene, the fairest
Ever burst on human view;
Once behold, and thou comparest
Nothing in the world thereto.

While the broad flood murmurs glistening
To the moon that hangeth listening
Moon that looketh down the sky,
Like an aloe-bloom on high

V
Sudden conch o'er the wave ringeth!
Ere the date-leaves cease to snake,
All, that hath existence, springeth
Into broad light, wide-awake.

As at a window of heaven thrown up,
All in a dazzling blaze are shown up,
Mellowing, ere our eyes avail,
To some soft enchanter's tale.

Every skiff a big ship seemeth,
Every bush with tall wings clad;
Every man his good brain deemeth
The only brain that is not mad.

VI
Hark! The pulse of measured rowing,
And the silver clarions blowing,
From the distant darkness, break
Into this illumined lake.

Tis Sesostris, lord of nations,
Victor of three continents,
Visiting the celebrations,
Priests, and pomps, and regiments.

Kings, from Indus, and Araxes,
Ister, and the Boreal axes,
Horsed his chariot to the waves,
Then embarked, his galley-slaves.

VII
Glittering stands the giant royal,
Four tall sons are at his back;
Twain, with their own corpses loyal,
Bridged the flames Pelusiac.

As he passeth, myriads bless him,
Glorious Monarch all confess him,
Sternly upright, to condone
No injustice, save his own.

He, well-pleased, his sceptre swingeth,
While his four sons strike the gong;
Till the sparkling water ringeth

Joy and laughter, joke and song.

VIII
Ah, but while loud merry-making
Sets the lights and shadows shaking,
While the mad world casts away
Every thought that is not gay,

Hath not earth, our sweet step-mother,
Very different scene hard by,
Tossing one, and trampling other,
Some to laugh, and some to sigh?

Where the fane of Hathor Iowereth,
And the black Myrike embowereth,
Weepeth one her life gone by;
Over young, oh death, to die!

IX
Nay, but lately she was yearning
To be quit of life's turmoil,
In the land of no returning,
Where all travel ends, and toil.

What temptations now entice her?
What hath made the world seem nicer?
Whence the charm, that strives anew
To prolong this last adieu?

Ah, her heart can understand it,
Though her tongue can ne'er explain:
Let yon granite Sphinx demand it
Riddle, ever solved in vain.

X
No constraint of hands hath bound her,
Not a chain hath e'er been round her;
Silver star hath sealed her brow,
Holy as an Isis cow.

Free to wander where she listeth;
No immurement must defile
(So the ancient law insisteth)
This, the hallowed bride of Nile.

What recks Abraham's descendant
Idols, priests, and pomps attendant?

And how long shall nature heed
What the stocks and stones decreed?

XI
"Fiendish superstitions hold thee
To a vile and hideous death.
Break their bonds; let love enfold thee;
Off, and fly with me;" he saith.

"Off! while priests are cutting capers
Priests of beetles, cats, and tapirs,
Brutes, who would thy beauty truck,
For an inch of yellow muck.

"Lo, my horse, Pyropus, yearneth
For the touch of thy light form;
Like the lightning, his eye burneth;
And his nostril, like the storm.

XII
"What are those unholy pagans?
Can they ride?   No more than Dagons.
Fishtails ne'er could sit a steed;
That belongs to Esau's seed.

"I will make thee Queen of far lands,
Flocks, and herds, and camel-trains,
Milk and honey, fruit and garlands,
Vines and venison, woods and wains.

"God is with us; He shall speed us;
Or (if this vile crew impede us)
Let some light into their brain,
By the sword of Tubal Cain."

XIII
"Nay," she answered, deeply sighing,
As the maid grew womanish
"Love, how hard have I been trying'
To believe the thing I wish!

"Thou hast taught me holy teachings,
Where to offer my beseechings,
Homage due to Heaven alone,
Not to ghosts, and graven stone,

"Thou hast shown me truth and freedom,

Love, and faith in One most High;
But thou hast not, Prince of Edom,
Taught me therewithal, to lie.

XIV
"Little cause had I for fretting,
None on earth to be regretting;
Till I saw thee, brave and kind;
And my heart undid my mind.

"Better, if the Gods had slain me,
When no difference could be;
Ere the joy had come to pain me,
And, alas, my dear one, thee!

"But shall my poor life throw shame on
Royal lineage of Amor?
Tis of Egypt's oldest strains;
Kingly blood flows in my veins.

XV
"Thou hast seen; my faith is plighted,
That I will not fly my doom.
Honour is a flower unblighted,
Though the fates cut off its bloom.

"I have sent my last sun sleeping,
And I am ashamed of weeping.
God, my new God, give me grace
To be worthy of my race.

"Though this death our bodies sever,
Thou shalt find me there above;
Where I shall be learning ever,
To be worthy of thy love."

XVI
From his gaze she turned, to borrow
Pride's assistance against sorrow
God vouchsafes that scanty loan,
When He taketh all our own.

Sudden thought of heaven's inspiring
Flashed through bold Duke Iram's heart;
Angels more than stand admiring,
When a man takes his own part.

'Tis the law the Lord hath taught us,
To undo what Satan wrought us;
To confound the foul fiend's plan,
With the manliness of man.

XVII
"Thou art right," he answered lowly,
As a youth should sneak a maid;
"Like thyself, thy word is holy;
Love is hate, if it degrade.

"But when thou hast well surrendered,
And thy sacrifice is tendered
God do so, and more to me,
If I slay not, who slay thee!

"Abraham's God hath ne'er forsaken
Them who trust in Him alway.
Thy sweet life shall not be taken.
Rest, and calm thee, while I pray."

XVIII
Like a little child, that kneeleth
To tell God whate'er he feeleth,
Bent the tall young warrior there,
And the palm-trees whispered prayer.

She, outworn with woe and weeping,
Shared that influence from above;
And the fear of death went sleeping
In the maiden faith and love.

Less the stormy water waileth,
E'en the human tumult faileth;
Stars their silent torches light,
To conduct the car of night

PART III

I
Lo, how bright-eyed morn awaketh
Tower and temple, nook and Nile;
How the sun exultant maketh
All the world return his smile!

O'er the dry sand, vapour twinkleth,

Like an eye when old age wrinkleth;
While, along the watered shore
Runs a river of gold ore.

Temple-front and court resemble
Mirrors swung in wavering light;
While the tapering columns tremble
At the view of their own height.

II
Marble shaft, and granite portal,
Statues of the Gods immortal
Quiver, with their figures bent,
In a liquid pediment

Thence the flood-leat followeth swiftly,
Where the peasant, spade in hand,
Guideth many a runnel deftly
Through his fruit and pasture-land;

Oft, the irriguous bank cross-slicing,
Plaited trickles he keeps enticing;
Till their gravelly gush he feels,
Overtaking his brown heels.

III
Life, that long hath born the test of
More than ours could bear, and live,
Springs anew, to make the best of
Every chance the Gods may give,

Doum-tree stiffeneth flagging feather;
Pate-leaves cease to cling together;
Citrons clear their welted rind;
Vines their mildewed sprays unwind.

Gourds, and melons, spread new lustre
On their veiny dull shagreen;
While the starred pomegranates cluster
Golden balls, with pink between.

IV
Yea, but heaven hath ordered duly,
Lest mankind should wax unruly,
Egypt, garner of all lore,
Narrow as a threshing-floor.

East, and West, lies desolation,
Infinite, untracked, untold
Shroud for all of God's creation,
When the wild blast lifts its fold;

There eternal melancholy
Maketh all delight unholy;
As a stricken widow glides
Past a group of laughing brides.

Who is this, that so disdaineth
Dome and desert, fear and fate;
While his jewell'd horse he reineth.
At Amen-Ra's temple-gate?

He, who crushed the kings of Asia,
Like a pod of colocasia;
Whom the sons of Anak fled,
Puling infants at his tread.

Who, with his own shoulders, lifted
Thrones of many a conquered land;
Who the rocks of Scythia rifted
King Sesostris waves his hand

VI
Blare of trumpet fills the valley;
Slowly, and majestically,
Swingeth wide, in solemn state,
Lord Amen-Ra's temple-gate.

Thence the warrior-host emeigeth,
Casque, and corselet, spear, and shield;
As the tide of red ore suigeth
From the furnace-door revealed.

After them, tumultuous rushing,
Mob, and medley, crowd, and crushing;
And the hungry file of priests,
Loosely zoned for larger feasts.

VII
"Look!" The whispered awe enhances
With a thrill their merry treat;
As one readeth grim romances,
In a sunny window-seat

"Look! It is the maid selected
For the sacrifice expected:
By the Gods, how proud and brave
Steps she to her watery grave!"

Strike up cymbals, gongs, and tabours,
Clarions, double-flutes, and drums;
All that bellows, or belabours,
In a surging discord comes.

VIII
Scarce Duke Iram can keep under
His wild steed's disdain and wonder,
While his large eyes ask alway
"Dareth man attempt to neigh?"

He hath snuffed the great Sahara,
And the mute parade of stars;
Shall he brook this shrill fanfara,
Ramshorns, pigskins, screechy jars?

What hath he to do with rabble?
Froth is better than their babble;
Let him toss them flakes of froth,
To pronounce his scorn and wrath.

IX
With his nostrils fierce dilating,
With his crest a curling sea,
All his volumed power is waiting
For the will, to set it free.

"Peace, my friend!"   The touch he knoweth
Calms his heart, howe'er it gloweth:
Horse can shame a man, to quell
Passion, where he loveth well.

"Nay, endure we," saith the rider,
"Till her plighted word be paid;
Then, though Satan stand beside her,
God shall help me swing this blade."

X
Lo, upon the deep-piled dais,
Wrought in hallowed looms of Sais,
O'er the impetuous torrent's swoop,
Stands the sacrificial group!

Tall High-priest, with zealot fires
Blazing in those eyeballs old,
Swathes him, as his rank requires,
Head to foot, in linen fold.

Seven attendants round him vying,
In a lighter vesture plying,
Four with skirts, and other three
Tunic'd short from waist to knee.

XI
Free among them stands the maiden,
Clad in white for her long rest;
Crowned with gold, and jewel-laden,
With a lily on her breast

Lily is the mark that showeth
Where that pure and sweet heart gloweth;
Here must come, to shed her life,
Point of sacrificial knife.

Here the knife is, cold and gleaming,
Here the colder butcher band.
Was the true love nought but dreaming,
Feeble heart, and coward hand?

XII
Strength unto the weak is given,
When their earthly bonds are riven;
Ere the spirit is called away,
Heaven begins its tranquil sway.

Life hath been unstained, and therefore
Pleasant to look back upon;
But there is not much to care for,
When the light of love is gone.

Still, though love were twice as fleeting,
Longeth she for one last greeting;
If her eyes might only dwell
Once on his, to say farewell

XIII
"Glorious Hapi," spake Piromis,
Lifting high his weapon'd hand;
"Earth thy footstool, heaven thy dome is,

We the pebbles on thy strand.

"Thou hast leaped the cubits twenty,
Dowering us with peace and plenty;
Mutha shows thee her retreat,
And the desert licks thy feet,

"We have passed through our purgation,
Once again we are thy kin;
God, accept our expiation,
Maiden pure of mortal sin."

XIV
"Ha!" the king cried, smiling blandly;
"Ha!" the trumpets answered grandly.
Proudly priest whirled, knife on high,
While the maiden bowed to die.

Sudden, through the ranks beside her,
Scattering men, like sparks of flint,
Burst a snow-white horse and rider,
Rapid as the lightning's glint.

One blow hurls Arch-priest to quiver
Headless, in his beloved river,
In the twinkling of an eye,
All the rest are dead, or fly.

XV
Iram, from Pyropus sweeping,
As a mower swathes the rye,
Caught his love, in terror sleeping,
And her light form swings on high.

"Soul of Khons!" Sesostris shouted,
Striding down the planks blood-grouted
Into his beard fell something light,
And he spat, and swooned with fright.

What hath made this great king stagger,
Reel, and shriek "unclean, unclean!"
Thunderbolt, or flash of dagger?
Nay, 'twas but a garden bean.

XVI
Brave Pyropus, blood-bespattered,
Snorts at men and corpses scattered,

Throws his noble chest more wide,
Leaps into the leaping tide.

Vainly hiss a thousand arrows,
Launched at random through the foam;
Every stroke the distance narrows
Twixt him and his desert home.

Sorely tried, and passion-shaken,
Long amid her foes forsaken,
Now, in tumult of surprise,
Lita knows not where she lies.

XVII
Till a bright wave breaks upon her,
And her clear perceptions wake
All his valour, prowess, honour,
Scorn of life, for her poor sake!

Gently then her eyes she raises,
(Eyes, whence all the pure soul gazes)
Softly brings her lips to his
Lips, wherein the whole heart is.

Let the furious waters welter,
Let the rough winds roar above;
Waves are warmth, and storms are shelter,
In the upper heaven of love.

XVIII
Fierce the flood, and wild the danger;
Yet the noble desert-ranger
Flinches not, nor flags, before
He hath brought them safe ashore.

Lives there man, who would have striven,
Reckless thus of storm and sword;
Leaped into the gulf, and given
Heart and soul, to please his Lord?

With caresses they have plied him,
Hand in hand they kneel beside him,
While their mutual vows they plight
To the God of life and light

XIX
Ha! What meaneth yon sword-flashing?

Trumps, and shouts from wave and isle?
Lo, the warrior galleys dashing,
To avenge insulted Nile!

Haste! The brave steed, leaping lightly,
'Neath his double burden sprightly,
Challenges, with scornful note,
Every horse in Pharaoh's boat.

King of Egypt, curb thy rages;
Lo, how trouble should be borne!
Memnon soothes the woe of ages,
With a sweet song, every morn.

KADISHA; OR, THE FIRST JEALOUSY
AN EASTERN LEGEND

HERE IS A CURIOUS LEGEND AS TO THE ORIGIN OP JEALOUSY. WHEN
ADAM AND EVE WERE IN PARADISE, THE FORMER WAS ACCUSTOMED TO
RETIRE AT EVENTIDE TO THE RECESSES OF THE GARDEN, FOR THE
PURPOSE OF PRAYER. ON ONE OF THESE OCCASIONS THE DEVIL
APPEARED TO EVE, AND INFORMED HER THAT HER SOLITUDE WAS TO
BE ACCOUNTED FOR BY THE ATTRACTIONS OF ANOTHER FAIR ONE. EVE
REPLIED THAT IT COULD NOT BE SO, AS SHE WAS THE ONLY WOMAN IN
EXISTENCE. "IF I SHOW YOU ANOTHER, WILL YOU BELIEVE ME?"
RETURNED THE EVIL ONE, AND PRODUCED A MIRROR, IN WHICH SHE
SAW HER OWN REFLECTION, AND MISTOOK IT FOR HER RIVAL.   See
"Life in Abyssinia," by Mr. Parkyns.
Murray, Albemarle Street.

The Kadisha, flowing to the south of Lebanon, is called "the holy river," as
having been a minor stream of Paradise.

PART I
True love's regale is incomplete,
'Till bitter leaven make it sweet;
Accept not then our tale amiss,
That jealousy was part of bliss;
But rather note a mercy here,
That fact was thus outrun by fear;
And so, before the harder bout,
When sin must be encountered too,
A woman's heart already knew
The way to conquer doubt

I

"When sleep was in the summer air,
And stars looked down on Paradise,
And palms and cedars answered fair
The visionary night-wind's sighs,
And murmuring prayer:

When every flower was in its hood
(By clasps of diamond dew retained),
Or sunk to elude Phalcena's brood,
Down slumber's breast with shadows veined,
In solitude:

The citron, stephanote, and rose,
Pomegranate, hoya, calycanth,
And yet unwanted amaranth,
Were sweetness in repose:

II
When rivulets were loth to creep,
Except unto the pillow moss,
And distant lake, encurtained deep,
Was but a silver thread across
The eyes of sleep:

When nightingales, in the sycamore,
Sang low and soft, as an echo dreaming;
And slept the moon upon heaven's shore
The tidal shore of heaven, beaming
With lazuled ore:

When new-born earth was fain to lean
In Summer's arms, recovering
The unaccustomed toil of Spring,
Why slept not Eve, their Queen?

III
Upon a smooth fern-mantled stone
She sat, and watched the wicket-gate,
Not timid in her woman's throne,
Nor lonely in her sinless state,
Though all alone;

For having spread her simple board
With grapes, and peaches, milk, and flowers,
She strewed sweet mastic o'er the sward,
And waited through the bridal hours
Step of her lord.

Such innocence around her breathed,
And freshness of young nature's play,
The sensitive plant shrank not away,
And cactus' swords were sheathed.

IV
The vision of her beauty fell,
Like music on a moonlit place,
Or trembles of a silver bell,
Or memories of a sacred face,
Too dear to tell:

The grace that wandered free of laws,
The look that lit the heart's confession,
Had never dreamed how fair it was;
Nor guessed that purity's expression
Is beauty's cause:

No more that unenquiring heart
Perused the sweet home of her breast,
Than turtle-doves unline their nest
To scan the outer part

V
Although, in all that garden fair,
Whate'er delight abode, or grew,
Flowers, and trees, and balmy air,
Fountains, and birds, and heaven blue
Beyond compare:

In her their various charms had met,
And grown more varied by combining,
As budded plants do give and get,
Each inmate doubling while resigning
His several debt:

And yet she nursed one joy, above
Her thousand charms, nor bora of them,
But blooming on a single stem
Her true faith in her love.

VI
And though, before she heard his foot,
The moon had climbed the homestead palm,
Flinging to her the shadowed fruit,
And tree-frogs ceased to break the calm,

And birds were mute,

With sudden transport ever new,
She blushed, and sprang from forth the bower,
Her eyes, as bright as moon-lit dew,
Her bosom glad as snow-veiled flower,
When sun shines through;

He, with a natural dignity
Untaught self-consciousness by harm,
Sustained her with his manly arm,
And smiled upon her glee.

VII
Next day, when early evening shone
Along the walks of Paradise,
Strewing with gold the hills, her throne,
Embarrassing the winds with spice
(Too rich a loan),

Fair Eve was in her bower of ease,
A cool arcade of fruit and flowers,

From North and East enclasped by trees,
But open to the Western showers,
And Southern breeze.

Here followed she her gardening trade,
Her favourites' simple needs attending,
And singing soft, above them bending,
A song herself had made.

VIII
In evening's calm, she walked between
The tints and shades of rich delight,
While overhead came, arching green,
Many a shrub and parasite,
To crown their Queen;

There laughed the joy of the rose, among
Myrtle and Iris, heaven's eye,
Magnole, with cups of moonlight hung,
And Fuchsia's sunny chandlery,
And coral tongue;

And where the shy brook fluttered through,
Nepenthe held her chalice leaf

(Undrained as yet by human grief),
And broad Nymphaea grew.

IX
But where the path bent towards the wood,
Across it hung a sombre screen,
The deadly night-shade, leaden-hued;
And there behind it, darkly seen,
A Being stood:

The form, if any form it had,
Was likest to a nightly vision
In mantle of amazement clad,
A terror-sense, without precision,
Of something bad.

A tremble chilled the forest shade,
A roving lion turned and fled,
The birds cowered home in hush of dread;
But Eve was not afraid.

X
She stood before him, sweetly bold,
To keep him from her garden shrine,
With hair that fell, a shower of gold,
Around her figure's snowy line
And rosy mould:

He (with a re-awakened sense
Of goodness, long for ever lost,
And angel beauty's pure defence)
Shrank back, unable to accost
Such innocence:

But envy soon scoffed down his shame;
And with a smile, designed for fawning,
But like hell's daybreak sickly dawning,
His crafty accents came.

XI
"Sweet ignorance, 'tis sad and hard
To break thy fond confiding spell;
And my soft heart hath such regard
For thine, that I will never tell
What may be spared."

He turned aside, o'erwhelmed with pain,

And drew a sigh of deep compassion:
She trembled, flushed, and gazed again,
And prayed him quick, in woman's fashion,
To speak it plain:

"Then, if thou must be taught to grieve,
And scorn the guile thou hast adored
The man who calls himself thy lord,
Where goes he, every eve?"

XII
"Nay, then," she cried, "if that be all,
I care not what thou hast to say;
The guile that lurks therein is small
My husband but retires to pray,
At evening call."

"To pray? Oh yes, and on his knees
May-hap to find a lovely being:
Devotions so devout as these
Are best at night, with no one seeing,
Among the trees."

She blushed as deep as modesty,
Then glancing back as bright as cride,
"What woman can he find,' she cried,
"In all the world, but me?"

XIII
He laughed with a superior sneer,
Enough to shake e'en woman's faith;
"Wilt thou believe me, simple dear,
If I am able now," he saith,
"To show her here?"

She cried aloud with gladsome heart,
"Be that the test whereon to try thee;
Nature and heaven shall take my part:
Come, show this rival; I defy thee
And all thy art."

A mirror, held in readiness,
He set upright before her feet
"Now can thy simple charms compete
With beauty such as this?"

XIV

A lovelier sight therein she saw
Than ever yet had charmed her eyes,
A fairer picture, void of flaw,
Than any, even Paradise
Itself, could draw;

A woman's form of perfect grace,
In shadowy softness delicate;
Though flushed by sunset's rich embrace,
A white rose could not imitate
Her innocent face:

Then, through the deepening glance of fear,
The shaft of doubt came quivering,
The sorrow-shaft, a sigh its wing,
And for its barb a tear.

XV
"Ah me!" she cried, "too true it is!
A simple homely thing, like Eve,
Hath not a chance to rival this,
But must resign herself to grieve
O'er by-gone bliss.

"Till now it was enough for me
To be what God our Father made;
Oh, Adam, I was proud to be
(As I have felt, and thou hast said)
A part of thee.

"No marvel that my lord can spare
His true and heaven-appointed bride.
And yet affection might have tried
To fancy me as fair."

XVI
The Tempter, glorying in his wile,
Hath ta'en his mirror and withdrawn;
Again the flowers look up and smile,
And brightens off from air and lawn
The taint of guile.

But smiles come not again to Eve,
Nor brightens off her dark reflection:
Her garland-crown she hath ceased to weave,
And, plucking, maketh no selection;
Only to grieve.

She feels a dewy radiance steep
The languid petals of her eyes,
And hath another sad surprise,
To know the way to weep,

PART II

The tears were still in woman's eyes,
When morn awoke on Paradise;
And still her sense of shame forbade
To tell her grievance, or upbraid;
Nor knew she which was dearer cost,
To seek him, or to shun him most
Then Adam, willing to believe
A heart by casual fancy moved
Would soon come back, at voice she loved,
Addressed his song to Eve.

I
"Come fairest, while the morn is fair,
And dews are bright as yon clear eyes;
Calm down this tide of troubled hair,
Forget with me all other sighs
Than summer air.

"Like me, the woodland shadows roam
At light (their fairer comrade's) side;
And peace and joy salute our home;
And lo, the sun in all his pride
My sunshine, come!

"The fawns and birds, that know our call,
Are waiting for our presence, see,
They wait my presence, love; and thee,
The most desired of all.

II
"The trees, which thought it grievous thing
To weep their own sweet leaves away,
Untaught as yet how soon the Spring
Upon their nestled heads should lay
Her callow wing

"The trees, whereat we smiled again,
To see them, in their growing wonder,

Suppose their buds were verdant rain,
Until the gay winds rustled under
Their feathered train,

"Lo, now they stand in braver mien,
And, claiming stronger shadow-right,
Make prisoner of the intrusive light,
And strew the winds with green.

III
"Of all the flowers that bow the head,
Or gaze erect on sun and sky,
Not one there is, declines to sned,
Or standeth up, to qualify
His incense-meed:

"Of all that blossom one by one,
Or join their lips in loving cluster,
Not one hath now resolved alone,
Or taken counsel, that his lustre
Shall be unshown.

"So let thy soul a blossom be,
To breathe the fragrance of its praise,
And lift itself, in early days,
To Him who fosters thee.

IV
"Of all the founts, bedropped with light,
Or silver-tress'd with shade of trees,
Not one there is, but sprinkles bright
It's plume of freshness on the breeze,
And jewelled flight:

"Of all that hush among the moss,
Or babble to the lily-vases,
Not one there is but purls across
A gush of the delight, that causes
It's limpid gloss.

"So let thy heart a fountain be,
To rise in sparkling joy, and fall
In dimpled melody and all
For love of home, and me."

V
The only fount her heart became

Rose quick with sighs, and fell in tears;
While pink upon her white cheek came,
(Like apple-blossom among pear's)
The tinge of shame.

Her husband, pierced with new alarm,
Bent nigh to ask of her distresses,
Enclasping her with sheltering arm,
Unwinding by discreet caresses,
The thread of harm.

Then she, with sobs of slow relief
(For silence is the jail of care)
Confessed, for him to heal or share,
The first of human grief.

VI
"I cannot look on thee, and think
That thou has ceased to hold me dear;
I cannot break the loosened link:
When thou, my only one, art near,
How can I shrink?

"So it were better, love, I mean,
My lord, it is more wise and right
That I, as one whose day hath been,
Should keep my pain from pleasure's sight,
And dwell unseen.

"And, though it break my heart to say
However sad my loneliness,
I fear thou wouldst rejoice in this
To have me far away.

VII
"I know not how it is with man,
Perhaps his nature is to change,
On finding consort fairer than
But oh, I cannot so arrange
My nature's plan!

"And haply thou hast never thought
To vex, or make me feel forsaken;
But, since to thee the thing was nought,
Supposed 'twould be as gaily taken,
As lightly brought.

"Yet, is it strange that I repine,
And feel abased in lonely woe,
To lose thy love or e'en to know
That half of it is mine?

VIII
"For whom have I on earth but thee,
What heart to love, or home to bless?
Albeit I was wrong, I see,
To think my husband took no less
Delight in me.

"But even now, if thou wilt stay,
Or try at least no more to wander,
And let me love thee, day by day,
Till time, or habit, make thee fonder
(If so it may)

"Thou shalt have one more truly bent,
In homely wise, on serving thee,
Than any stranger e'er can be;
And Eve shall seem content."

IX
Not loud she wept but hope could hear;
Sweet hope, who in his lifelong race
Made terms, to win the goal from fear,
That each alternate step should trace
A smile and tear.

But Adam, lost in wide amaze,
Regarded her with troubled glances,
Misdoubting 'neath her steady gaze,
Himself to be in strange romances,
And dreamy haze:

Then questioning in hurried voice,
And scarcely waiting her replies,
He spoke, and showed the true surprise
That made her soul rejoice.

X
She told him what the Tempter said,
And what her frightened self had seen,
(That form in loveliness arrayed,
With modest face, and graceful mien)
And how displayed.

Then well-content to show his bride
The worldly knowledge he possessed,
(That world whereof was none beside)
He laid his hand upon his breast,
And thus replied:

"Wife, mirror'd here too deep to see,
"A little way down yonder path,
"And I will show the form which hath
"Enchanted thee, and me."

XI
Kadisha is a streamlet fair,
Which hurries down the pebbled way,
As one who hath small time to spare,
So far to go, so much to say
To summer air;

Sometimes the wavelets wimple in
O'erlapping tiers of crystal shelves,
And little circles dimple in,
As if the waters quaffed themselves,
The while they spin:

Thence in a clear pool, overbent
With lotus-tree and tamarind flower,
Empearled, and lulled in golden bower,
Kadisha sleeps content.

XII
Their steps awoke the quiet dell;
The first of men was smiling gay;
Still trembled Eve beneath the spell,
The mystery of that passion-sway
She could not quell.

As they approached the silver strand,
He plucked a moss-rose budding sweetly,
And wreathing bright her tresses' band,
Therein he set the blossom featly,
And took her hand:

He led her past the maiden-hair,
Forget-me-not, and meadow-sweet,
Until the margin held her feet,
Like water-lilies fain

XIII
"Behold," he cried, "on yonder wave,
The only one with whom I stray,
The only image still I have,
Too often, even while I pray
To Him who gave.

The form she saw was long unknown,
Except as that beheld yestreen;
Till viewing, not that form alone,
But his, with hands enclasped between,
She guessed her own.

And, bending o'er in sweet surprise,
Perused, with simple child's delight,
The flowing hair, and forehead white,
And soft inquiring eyes.

XIV
Then, blushing to a fairer tint
Than waves might ever hope to catch,
"I see," she cried, "a lovely print;
But surely I can never match
This lily glint!

"So pure, so innocent, and bright,
So charming free, without endeavour,
So fancy-touched with pensive light I
I think that I could gaze forever,
With new delight

"And now that rose-bud in my hair,
Perhaps it should be placed above
And yet, I will not change it, love,
Since mou hast set it there.

XV
"Vain Eve, why glory thus in Eve?
What matter Tor thy form or face?
Thy beauty is, if love believe
Thee worthy of that treasured place
Thou ne'er shalt leave.

"Oh, husband; mine and mine alone,
Take back my faith that dared to wander;
Forgive my joy to have thee shown

Not transient, as thine image yonder,
But all my own.

"And, love, if this be vain of me,
This pleasure, and the pride I take;
Tis only for thy dearer sake,
To be so fair to thee."

XVI
No more she said; but smiling fell,
And lost her sorrow on his breast;
Her love-bright eyes upon him dwell,
Like troubled waters laid at rest
In comfort's well:

Tis nothing more, an' if she weep,
Than joy she cannot else reveal;
As onyx-gems of Pison keep
A tear-vein, where the sun may steal
Throughout their deep.

May every Adam's fairer part
Thus, only thus, a rival find
The image of herself, enshrined
Within the faithful heart!

MOUNT ARAFA

IN TWO PARTS

"Mount Arafa, situated about a mile from Mecca, is held in great
veneration by the Mussulmans, as a place very proper for penitence. Its
fitness in this respect is accounted for by a tradition that Adam and Eve,
on being banished out of Paradise, in order to do penance for their
transgression were parted from each other, and after a separation of six
score years, met again upon this mountain." Ockley's "History of the
Saracens," p. 60

THE PARTING
I
Driven away from Eden's gate
With biasing falchions fenced about,
Into a desert desolate,
A miserable pair came out,

To meet their fate.

To wander in a world of woe,
To ache and starve, to burn and shiver,
With every living thing their foe
The fire of God above, the river
Of death below.

Of home, of hope, of Heaven bereft;
It is the destiny of man
To cower beneath his Maker's ban,
And hide from his own theft!

II
The father of a world unborn
Who hath begotten death, ere life
In sullen silence plods forlorn;
His love and pride in his fair wife
Are rage and scorn.

Instead of Angel ministers,
What hath he now but fiends devouring;
Instead of grapes and melons, burs;
In lieu of manna, crab and souring
By whose fault?   Hers!

Alack, good sire of feeble knees,
New penance waits thee; since when thus
Thou shouldst have wept for all of us
Thou mournest thine own ease I

III
The mother of all loving wives
(Condemned unborn to many a tear)
Is fain to take his hand, and strives
In sorrow to be doubly dear
But shame deprives.

The shame, the woe, the black surprise,
That love's first dream should have such ending,
To weep, and wipe neglected eyes I
Oh loss of true love, far transcending
Lost Paradise!

For is it faith, that cannot live
One gloomy hour, and soar above
The clouds of fate?   And is it love,

That will not e'en forgive?

IV
The houseless monarch of the earth
Hath quickly found what empire means;
For while he scoffs with bitter mirth,
And curses, after Eden's scenes,
This dreary dearth.

A snake, that twined in playful zeal,
But yester morn, around his ankle,
Now driven along the dust to steal,
Steals up, and leaves its venom'd rankle
Deep in his heel.

He groans awhile.   He seeks anon
For comfort to this first of pain,
Where all his sons to-day are fain;
He seeks but Eve is gone!

PART I - ADAM
O'er hill, and highland, moor, and plain,
A hundred years, he seeks in vain;
Oer hill and plain, a hundred years,
He pours the sorrow no one hears;
Yet finds, as wildest mourners find,
Some ease of heart in toil of mind.

I
"Ye mountains, that forbid the day,
Ye glens, that are the steps of night,
How long amid you must I stray,
Deserted, banished from God's sight,
And castaway?

"Ye trees and flowers the Lord hath made,
Ye beasts, to my good-will committed
Although your trust hath been betrayed
Not long ago ye would have pitied
Your old comrade.

"Oh, nature, noblest when alone,
Albeit I love your outward part;
The nature that enthrals my heart
Must be more like my own.

II

"The Maker once appointed me
I know not, and I care not why
The lord of everything I see,
Or if they walk, or swim, or fly,
Whate'er they be.

"And all the earth whereon they dwell,
And all the heavens they are inhaling,
And powers, whereof I cannot tell
Dark miscreants, supine and wailing,
Until I fell.

"Twas good and glorious to believe;
But now mv majesty is o'er;
And I would give it all, and more,
For one sweet glimpse of Eve.

III

"For what is glory, what is power?
And what the pride of standing first?
A twig struck down by a thunder shower,
A crown of thistle to quench the thirst,
A sun-scorched flower.

"God grant the men who spring from me,
As knowledge waxeth deep and splendid,
To find a loftier pedigree
Than any by the Lord intended
Frog, slug, or tree!

"So shall they live, without the grief
Of having womankind to love,
Find nought below, and less above,
And be their own belief.

IV

"So weak was I, so poorly taught,
By any but my Maker's voice,
Too happy to indulge in thought,
Which gives me Tittle to rejoice,
And ends in nought.

"But now and then, my path grows clear,
My mind casts off its grim confusion,
When I have chanced on goodly cheer:
Then happiness seems no delusion,

Even down here.

"With love and faith, to bless the curse,
To heal the mind by touch of heart,
To make me feel my better part,
And fight against the worse.

V
"It may be that I did o'erprize,
Above the Giver, that rare gift,
Ungird my will for softer ties,
And hold my manhood little thrift
To woman's eyes.

"So far she was, so full of grace,
So innocent with coy caresses,
So proud to step at my own pace,
So rosy through her golden tresses;
And such a face!

"Suffice my sins; I'll ne'er approve
A thought against my faithful Eve;
Suffice my sins; I'll never believe.
That it was one, to love.

VI
"Oh; love, if e'er this desert plain,
Where I must sweat with axe and spade,
Shall hold a people sprung from twain,
Or better made by Him, who made
That pair in vain.

"Shall any know, as we have known,
Thy rapture, terror, vaunting, fretting,
Profound despair, ecstatic tone,
Crowning of reason, and upsetting
Of reason's throne?

"Bright honey quaffed from cells of gall,
Or crimson sting from creamy rose
Thy heavenly half from Eden flows,
Thy venom from our fall."

Awhile he ceased; far scorching woe
Had made a drought of vocal flow;
When hungry, weary, desolate,
A fox crept home to his defis gate.

The sight brought Adam's memory back,
And touched him with a keener lack.

VII
"Home! Where is home? Of old I thought
(Or felt in mystery of bliss)
That so divinely was I wrought
As not to care for that or this,
And value nought;

"But sit or saunter, rest or roam,
Regarding all things most sublimely,
As if enthroned on heaven's dome;
Away with paltry and untimely
Hankerings for Home!

"But now the weary heart is fain
For shelter in some lowly nest
To sink upon a softer breast,
And smile away its pain,

VIII
"For me, what home, what hope is left?
What difference of good or ill?
Of all I ever loved bereft,
Disgraced, discarded, outlawed still,
For one small theft!

"I sicken of my skill and pride;
I work, without a bit of caring.
The world is waste, the world is wide;
Why make good things, with no one sharing
Them at my side?

"What matters how I dwell, or die?
Away with such a niggard life!
The Lord hath robbed me of my wife;
And life is only I.

IX
"God, who hast said it is not good
For man, thy son, to live alone;
Is everlasting solitude,
When once united bliss was known,
A livelier food?

"Can'st thou suppose it right or just,

When thine own creature so misled us,
In virtue of our simple trust,
To torture us like this, and tread us
Back into dust?

"Oh, fool I am. Oh, rebel worm!
If, when immortal, I was slain,
For daring to impugn his reign,
How shall I, thus infirm?

X
"Woe me, poor me! No humbler yet,
For all the penance on me laid!
Forgive me, Lord, if I forget
That I am but what Thou hast made,
My soul Thy debt!

"Inspire me to survey the skies,
And tremble at their golden wonder;
To learn the space that I comprise,
At once to marvel, and to ponder,
And drop mine eyes.

"And grant me? for I do but find,
In seeking more than God hath shown,
I scorn His power and lose my own
Grant me a lowly mind.

XI
"A lowly mind! Thou wondrous sprite,
Whose frolics make their master weep;
Anon, endowed with eagle's flight,
Anon, too impotent to creep,
Or blink aright;

"Howe'er, thy trumpery flashes play
Among the miracles above thee,
Be taught to feel thy Maker's sway,
To labour, so that He shall love thee,
And guide thy way.

"Be led, from out the cloudy dreams
Of thy too visionary part,
To listen to the whispering heart,
And curb thine own extremes.

XII

"Then hope shall shine from heaven, and give
To fruit of hard work, sunny cheek,
And flowers of grace and love revive,
And shrivelled pasturage grow sleek,
And corn snail thrive.

"Beholding gladness, Eve and I,
Enfolding it also in each other,
May talk of heaven without a sigh;
Because our heaven in one another
Love shall supply.

"For courage, faith, and bended knees,
By stress of patience, cure distress,
And turn wild Love-in-idleness
Into the true Heartsease."

The Lord breathed on the first of men,
And strung his limbs to strength again;
He scorned a century of ill,
And girt his loins to climb the parting hill.

PART II - EVE
Meanwhile through lowland, holt, and glade,
Sad Eve her lonely travel made;
Not fierce, or proud, but well content
To own the righteous punishment;
Yet found, as gentle mourners find,
The hearts confession soothe the mind.

I
"Ye valleys, and ye waters vast,
Who answer all that look on you
With shadows of themselves, that last
As long as they, and are as true
Where hath he past?

"Oh woods, and heights of rugged stone,
Oh weariness of sky above me,
For ever must I pine and moan,
With none to comfort, none to love me,
Alone, alone?

"Thou bird, that hoverest at heaven's gate,
Or cleavest limpid lines of air,
Return, for thou hast one to care

Return to thy dear mate.

II
"For trie, no joy of earth or sky,
No commune with the things I see,
But dreary converse of the eye
With worlds too grand to look at me
No smile, no sigh!

"In vain I fall Upon my knees,
In vain I weep and sob for ever;
All other miseries have ease,
All other prayers have ruth but never
Any for these.

"Are we endowed with heavenly breath,
And God's own form, that we should win
A proud priority of sin,
And teach creation death?

III
"Not, that is too profound for me,
Too lofty for a fallen thing.
More keenly do I feel than see;
Far liefer would I, than take wing,
Beneath it be.

"The night, the dark, will soon be here,
The gloom that doth my heart appal so I
How can I tell what may be near?
My faith is in the Lord, but also
He hath made fear.

"I quail, I cower, I strive to flee;
Though oft I watched without affright,
The stern magnificence of night,
When Adam was with me

IV
"My husband! Ah, I thought sometime
That I could do without him well,
Communing with the heaven at prime,
And in my womanhood could dwell
Calm and sublime.

"Declining, with a playful strife,
All thoughts below my own transcendence,

All common-sense of earth and life,
And counting it a poor dependence
To be his wife,

"But now I know, by trouble's test,
How little my poor strength can bear,
What folly wisdom is, whene'er
The grief is in the breast!

"The grief is in my breast, because
I have not always been as kind
As woman should, by nature's laws,
But showed sometimes a wilful mind,
Carping at straws.

"While he, perhaps, with larger eyne,
Was pleased, instead of vexed, at seeing
Some little petulance in mine,
And loved me all the more, for being;
Not too divine.

"Until the pride became a snare,
The reason a deceit, wherein
I dallied face to face with sinh
And made a mortal pair.

VI
"Dark sin, the deadly foe of love,
All bowers of bliss thou shalt infest,
Implanting thorns the flowers above,
And one black feather in the breast
Of purest dove.

"Almighty Father, once our friend,
And ready even now to love us.
Thy pitying gaze upon us bend,
And through the tempest-clouds above us
Thine arm extend.

"That so thy children may begin
In lieu of bliss, to earn content,
And find that sinful Eve was meant
Not only for a sin."

Awhile she ceased; for memory's flow
Had drowned the utterance of woe;
Until a young hind crossed the lawn,

And fondly trotted forth her fawn,
Whose frolics of delight made Eve,
As in a weeping vision, grieve.

VII
"For me, poor me, no hope to learn
That sweeter bliss than Paradise,
The joy that makes a mother yearn
O'er that bright message from the skies
Her pains do earn.

She stoops entranced; she fears to stir,
Or think; lest each a thought endanger
(While two enraptured hearts confer)
That wonderful and wondering stranger,
Come home to her,

"He watches her, in solemn style;
A world of love flows to and fro;
He smiles; that he may learn to know
His mother by her smile.

VIII
"Oh, bliss, that to all other bliss
Shall be as sunrise unto night,
Or heaven to such a place as this,
Or God's own voice, with angels bright,
To serpent's hiss!

"I have I betrayed thee, or cast by
The pledge in which my soul delighted
That all this wrong and misery
Should be avenged at last, and righted,
And so should I?

"Belike, they look on me as dead,
Those fiends that found me soft and sweet;
But God hath promised me one treat
To crush that serpent's head!

IX
"Revenge! Oh, heaven, let someone rise,
Some woman, since revenge is small,
Who shall not care about its size,
If only she can get it all,
For those black lies!

"Poor Adam is too good and great,
I felt it, though he said so little
To hate his foes, as I can hate
And pay them every jot, and tittle,
At their own rate.

"For was there none but I to blame?
God knows that if, instead of me,
There had been any other she,
She would have done the same,

X
"Poor me! Of course the whole disgrace,
In spite of reason, falls on me:
And so all women of my race,
In pure right, shall be reason-free,
In every case.

"It shall not be in power of man
To bind them to their own contentions;
But each shall speak, as speak she can,
And start anew with fresh inventions,
Where she began.

"And so shall they be dearer still;
For man shall ne'er suspect in them
The plucking of the fatal stem,
That brought him all his ill.

XI
"And when hereafter, as there must,
Since He, that made us, so hath sworn
From that whereof we are, the dust,
And whereunto we shall return
In higher trust

"There spring a grand and countless race,
Replenishing this vast possession,
Till life, hath won a larger space
Than death, by quick and fair succession
Of health and grace;

"They too shall find as I have found
The grief, that lifts its head on high,
A dewy bud the sun shall dry
But not while on the ground.

XII
"Then men shall love their wives again,
Allowing for the frailer kind,
Content to keep the heart's Amen,
Content to own the turns of mind
Beyond their ken.

"And wives shall in their lords be blest,
Their higher sense of right perceiving
(When possible) with love their test;
Exalting, solacing, believing
All for the test.

"And for the best shall all things be,
If God once more will shine around,
And lift my husband from the ground,
And teach him to lift me."

New faith inspired the first of wives,
She smiles, and drooping hope revives;
She scorns a hundred years of woe%
And binds her hair, because the breezes blow.

THE MEETING
I
The wind is hushed, the moon is bright,
More stars on heaven than may be told;
Young flowers are coying with the light,
That softly tempts them to unfold,
And trust the night.

What form comes bounding from above
Down Arafa, the mountain lonely,
Afraid to scare its long-lost dove,
Yet swift as joy "It can be only,
Only my love!"

What shape is that, too fair to leave
On Arafa, the mountain lone?
So trembling, and so faint, "My own,
It must be my own Eve!"

II
As when the mantled heavens display
The glory of the morning glow,
And spread the mountain heights with day,

And bid the clouds and shadows go
Trooping away,

The Spirit of the Lord arose,
And made the earth and heaven to quiver,
And scattered all his hellish foes,
And deigned his good stock to deliver
From all their woes.

So long the twain had strayed apart,
That each as at a marvel gazed,
With eyes abashed, and brain amazed;
While heart enquired of heart.

III
Our God hath made a fairer thing
Than fairest dawn of summer day
A gentle, timid, fluttering,
Confessing glance, that seeks alway
Rest for its wing.

A sweeter sight than azure skies,
Or golden star thereon that glideth;
And blest are they who see it rise,
For, if it cometh, it abideth
In woman's eyes.

The first of men such blessing sued;
The first of women smiled consent;
For husband, wife and home it meant,
And no more solitude!

IV
We trample now the faith of old,
We make our Gods of dream and doubt;
Yet life is but a tale untold,
Without one heart to love, without
One hand to hold

The fairer half of humankind,
More gentle, playful, and confiding:
Whose soul is not the slave of mind,
Whose spirit hath a nobler guiding
Than we can find.

So Eve restores the sweeter part
Of what herself unwitting stole,

And makes the wounded Adam whole;
For half the mind is heart.

THE WELL OF SAINT JOHN

The old well of Saint John, in the parish of Newton-Nottage,
Glamorganshire, has a tide of its own, which appears to run exactly
counter to that of the sea, some half-mile away. The water is
beautifully bright and fresh, and the quaint dome among the lonely
sands is regarded with some awe and reverence.

He
"THERE is plenty of room for two in here,
Within the steep tunnel of old grey stone;
And the well is so dark, and the spring so clear,
It is quite unsafe to go down alone."

She
"It is perfectly safe, depend upon it,
For a girl who can count the steps, like me;
And if ever I saw dear mother's bonnet,
It is there on the hill by the old ash-tree."

He
"There is nobody but Rees Hopkin's cow
Watching, the dusk on the milk-white sea;
'Tis the time and the place for a life-long? vow,
Such as I owe you, and you owe me."

She
"Oh, Willie, how can I, in this dark well?
I shall drop the brown pitcher if you let go;
The long? roof is murmuring like a sea-shell,
And the shadows are shuddering to and fro."

He
"'Tis the sound of the ebb, in Newton Bay,
Quickens the spring, as the tide grows less;
Even as true love flows alway
Counter the flood of the world's success."

She
"There is no other way for love to flow,
Whenever it springs in a woman's breast;
With the tide of its own heart it must go,
And run contrary to all the rest."

He
"Then fill the sweet cup of your hand, my love,
And pledge me your maiden faith thereon,
By the touch of the letter'd stone above,
And the holy water of Saint John."

She
"Oh, what shall I say?   My heart sinks low;
My fingers are cold, and my hand too flat,
Is love to be measured by handfuls so;
And you know that I love you without that."

They stooped, in the gleam of the faint light, over
The print of themselves on the limpid gloom;
And she lifted her full palm toward her lover,
With her lips preparing the words of doom.

But the warm heart rose, and the cold hand fell,
And the pledge of her faith sprang sweet and clear,
From a holier source than the old Saint's well,
From the depth of a woman's love, a tear.

PAUSIAS AND GLYCERA; OR, THE FIRST FLOWER-PAINTER
A STORY IN THREE SCENES

Scene I: Outside the gate of Sicyon - Morning. Glycera weaving garlands,
Pausias stands admiring.

Pausias
"Ye Gods, I thought myself the Prince of Art,
By Phoebus, and the Muses set apart,
To smite the critic with his own complaint,
And teach the world the proper way to paint.
But lo, a young maid trips out of a wood,
And what becomes of all I understood?

I stand and stare; I could not draw a line,
If ninety Muses came, instead of nine.
Thy name, fair maiden, is a debt to me;
Teach him to speak, whom thou hast taught to see.
Myself already some repute have won,
For I am Pausias, Brietes' son.
To boast behoves me not, nor do I need,
But often wish my friends to win the meed.
So shall they now; no more will I pursue

The beaten track, but try what thou hast shown,
New forms, new curves, new harmonies of tone,
New dreams of heaven, and how to make them true."

Glycera
"Fair Sir, 'tis only what I plucked this morn,
Kind nature's gift, ere you and I were born.
Through mossy woods, and watered vales, I roam,
While day is young, and bring my treasure home;
Each lovely bell so tenderly I bear,
It knoweth not my fingers from the air,
Lo now, they scarce acknowledge their surprise,
And how the dewdrops sparkle in their eyes!"

Pausias
"Because the sun shines out of thine.   But hush,
To praise a face praiseworthy, makes it blush.
I am not of the youths who find delight,
In every pretty thing that meets their sight
My father is the sage of Sicyon;
And I, well, he is proud of such a son."

Glycera
"And proud am I, my mother's child to be,
And earn for her the life she gave to me,
Her name is Myrto of the silver hair,
Not famed for wisdom, but loved everywhere."

Pausias
"Then whence thine art? Hath Phoebus given thee boon
Of wreath and posy, fillet and festoon?
Of tint and grouping, balance, depth, and tone
Lo, I could cast my palette down, and groan!"

Glycera
"No art, fair sir, hath ever crossed my thought,
The lesson I delight in comes untaught.
The flowers around me take their own sweet way,
They tell me what they wish and I obey.
Unlike poor us, they feel no spleen or spite
But earn their joy, oy ministering delight.
So loved and cherished, each may well suppose
Itself at home again just where it grows.
No dread have they of what the Fates may bring,
But trust their Gods, and breathe perpetual Spring."

Pausias

"Fair child of Myrto, simple-hearted maid,
Thy innocence doth arrogance upbraid.
Ye Gods, I pray you make a flower of me;
That I may dwell with nature, and with thee."

Glycera
"I see the brave sun leap the city wall!
The gates swing wide; I hear the herald's call.
The Archon ham proclaimed the market-day;
And mother will shed tears at my delay.
The priest of Zeus hath ordered garlands three;
And while I tarry, who will wait for me?"

Pausias
"No picture have I sold for many a moon,
But fortune must improve her habits soon;
Then will I purchase all thy stock-in-trade,
And thou shalt lead me to thy bower of green,
There will I paint the flowers, and thee their Queen
The Queen of dowers, that nevermore shall fade."

Glycera
"I know a wood-nymph, who her dwelling hath
Among the leaves, and far beyond the path,
With myrtle and with jasmin roofed across,
Enlaced with vine, and carpeted with moss,
Whose only threshold is a plaited brook,
Whereby the primrose at herself may look;
While birds of song melodious make the air
But oh! I must not take a stranger there."

Pausias
"Nay, but a friend   No stranger now am I.
Good art is pledge of perfect modesty.
From chastened heights the painter glanceth down;
No maid can fear a youth who loves renown."

Glycera
"Thy words are trim, If mother deems them true,
Thou shalt come with me. But till then, adieu!" [Exit.

Pausias
"O! where am I?   The mind is all for art
But one warm breath transforms it into heart."

Scene II: A wood near Sicyon. Pausias with his easel, &c. Glycera carrying flowers.

Pausias
"Confounded tangle!   Who could paint all this?
A bear might hug him, or a serpent hiss!
For love of nature justly am I famed;
But when she goes so far as this, she ought to be ashamed."

Glycera
"Nay, be not frightened by a small affray,
Pure love of nature cannot pave its way.
But lo, where yonder coney-tracks begin,
My nymph hath made her favourite bower within.
Yon oak hath reared its rugged antlers thus,
Before Deucalion lived, or Daedalus.
Inside her woodland Majesty doth keep
A world of wonders, if one dared to peep
Of things that burrow, elide, spin webs, or creep;
Strange creatures, which before they live must die,
And plants that hunt for prey, and flowers that fly!"

Pausias
"My love of nature freezes in a trice;
I loathe all earwigs, beetles, and wood-lice.
Outside her bower the lady must remain,
If she doth wish to have her portrait taen."

Glycera
"Tis not the lady thou must paint, but me."

Pausias
"Aha, that will I, with a glow of glee.
But when I offered, somebody was vexed,
And blushed, and frowned, and longed to say,
'Whatnext?'"

Glycera
"A painter's tongue hath learnt to paint, I trow.
But oh that order, I remember now
For twenty chaplets, from the priest of Zeus!
Ah, what a grand majestic Hiereus!"
So pleased he was that morning with those three,
And such a customer he means to be!

Pausias
"The priest of Dis!a scoundrel with three wives!

I'll pull his triple beard, if he arrives."

Glycera
"High words and threats profane this hallowed place,
Where Time rebukes the fuss of human race.
And gentle sir, what harm hath he done thee?
It is my mother whom he comes to see.
Lo, how the Gods our puny wrath deride,
With peace and beauty spread on every side!
This earth with pleasure of the Spring complete,
Too bright to dwell on, were it not so sweet.
No theft of man it's affluence impairs,
A thousand flowers, without a loss, it spares;
Whose bashful elegance no brush can trace,
Heartfelt delight, and plenitude of grace;
No palettes match their brilliance, although
Pandora filled her box from Iris' bow."

Pausias
"Her want of faith sweet Glycera will rue,
When she hath seen what Pausias can do."

Glycera
"Forgive me, sir; In truth it was no taunt.
A great man can do anything but vaunt."

Pausias
"E'en that he can do, if he sees the need.
But out on words, when time hath come for deed!
Up leaps the sun, to paint thee with his plume,
And every blossom seems to be thy bloom."

Glycera
"Why stand we here, so early of the morn,
In love with things that treat our love with scorn
Grey crags, where Time with folded pinion broods,
Ana ever young antiquity of woods;
The brooks that babble, and the flowers that blush,
Ere woman was a reed, or man a rush?
And he for ever, as the Gods ordain,
Would fain revive with art what he hath slain;
Shall nature fail to laugh, while man doth yearn
To teach the canvas what he ne'er can learn?"

Pausias
"Sweet Muse, while thus through heaven's too distant vault,
Thy great mind roves, how shall we earn our salt?

Though art is not encouraged as of old,
She is worth a score of nature; I design
To manufacture, from these flowers of thine,
A silver talent or perhaps of gold!"

Glycera
"Good heavens, how precious is your Worship's time!
Some minds are lowly, others too sublime.
Before thee all my simple flowers I spread;
Long may they live, when Glycera is dead!"

Pausias
"The Gods forefend!
Fair omen from fair maid
Bright tongue, recall the dark thing thou hast said!"

Glycera
"Then long live they, with Glycera to aid!"

Pausias
"And Pausias crowned by Critics, to non-plus
Euphranor, Cydias, and Antidotus.
But what are they?   Below my feet they lie;
Poor sons of pelf.   The son of art am I.
Now rest thee, maiden, on this pillowy bed,
With fragrance canopied, with beauty spread;
Above thee hovers eglantine's caress,
Around thee glows entangled loveliness;
Shy primrose smiles, thy gentle smile to woo,
And violets take thy glances for the dew."

&Glycera&
"Then will they pluck themselves, to see me laugh;
Good flowers bring cash; but who will pay for chaff?
But haply thus the true poet intervenes,
To make us wonder what on earth he means."

Pausias
"A poet! We do things in a superior way;
A painter is a poet, who makes it pay.
A poet, though deep and mystic as the Sphinx,
Will ne'er earn half of what he eats and drinks,
He dreams of Gods, but of himself he thinks."

Scene III. A western slope near Sicyon. Pausias has his easel set, Glycera
is dressed in white.

Pausias
"Seven times the moon hath filled her silver horn,
And twice a hundred suns awoke the morn,
Since thou and I, for half the praise is thine
Began this study of the flowers divine."

Glycera
"Alas! how swiftly have the months gone by!"

Pausias
"Not swift alone, but passing sweet for me."

Glycera
"The world, that was so large, is you and I."

Pausias
"And shall be larger still, when it is 'We.'"

Glycera
 (Aside) "Sweet dual! Alas, that this shall never be!"

Pausias
"A tear, bright Glycera in those eyes of thine,
Those tender eyes, that should with triumph shine!
When I, the owner of that precious heart,
Am shouting Iö Pæan of high art;
The noblest picture underneath the sun
A few more strokes, and victory is won!"

Glycera
"Nay, heed me not. True pleasure is not dry;
The sunrise of the heart bedews the eye."

Pausias
"If that were all, but lately there hath been
A listless air beneath thy livery mien;
Thyself art all fair petal, and sweet perfume,
And smiles that light the damask of thy bloom;
Yet some, pale distance seems to chill the whole."

Glycera
"Forgive me, love, forgive a timorous soul.
Through brightest hours untimely vapours rise
But while I prate, the lucky moment flies.
The work, the weather, and the world are fair;
A few more strokes and fame flies everywhere."

Pausias
"Who cares for fame, except with love to share?"

Glycera
"To share! Nay every breath of it is mine,
Whene'er it breathes on thee; for I am thine.
But pardon now, if I have seemed sometime
Impatient, glib, too pert for things sublime,
Remember that I meant not so to sink;
Forgive your Glycera, when you come to think."

Pausias
"I'll not forgive my Glycera, until
She hath discovered how to do some ill.
Now don once more this coronet of bloom,
While lilies sweet thy sweeter breast illume."

Glycera
 (Aside) "Ah me, what brightness wasted upon gloom!
(Aloud) Oh fling thy sponge across this wretched face,
A patch uncouth amid a world of grace."

Pausias
"Sweet love, thy beauty far outshineth them;
The tinsel they are, thou the living gem.
Great gift of Gods! Shall flowers of earth despise
Those flowers of heaven, thy tresses, and thine eyes?
Away with gloom I let no ill-boding make
My heart to falter, or my hand to shake.
One hour is all I crave. If that be long,
Sweet lips beguile it with my favourite song."

Glycera
"A song like mine, a childish lullaby,
Will close, when needed wide-awake, thine eye.
But since thou so demandest, let me try.

"In the fresh woods have I been,
Sprinkled with the morning dew;
And of all that I have seen,
Lo, the fairest are for you!

Take your choice of many a flower,
Lily, rose, and melilot,
Lilac, myrtle, virgin's bower,
Pansy, and forget-me-not.

Ladies'-tresses, and harebell,
Jasmin, daphne, violet,
Meadow-sweet, and pimpernel,
Maidenhair, and mignonette.

What is gold, that doth allure
Foolish hearts from field and flower?
If you plant them in it pure,
Will they keep alive an hour?

What is fame, compared with these,
Fame of wisdom, sword, or pen?
Who would quit the meadow breeze,
For the sultry breath of men?

These have been my childhood's love,
These my maiden visions were;
When I meet their gaze above,
These will tell me, God is there."

Pausias
"'Tis done!   No more the palsied doubt molests;
The crown of glory on my labour rests.
Thy clear voice hath my flagging thoughts supplied,
My model thou, my teacher, and my bride!
Now stand, beloved one, where the soft glow lies,
Yet judge not rashly, ere the colour dries.
Find every fault, pick every flaw thou canst;
I'll not be vexed; true art is thus advanced.
So meek is art, that (when it comprehends)
It loves the carping of its dearest friends.
If my own bride condemns my efforts, let her.
A poor daub? Well let someone do it better."

Glycera
"My love, my lord, my monarch of high art,
Forgive a tongue held fast and bound by heart.
Not Orpheus, Linus, or great Hermes could
Find words to make their rapture understood.
No Muse, no Phoebus, hath this work inspired,
But Jove himself, with heaven's own splendour fired.
I see the nursing fingers of the day,
And night as well, upon their offspring play
The silent glide of moon, that hushed their sleep,
(As mother at her infant steals a peep)
Anon, with pearly glances half withdrawn,

The gentle hesitation of the dawn;
I see the sun his golden target raise,
And drive in tremulous ranks the woodland haze;
Awakened by whose call the flowers arise,
With tears of joy and blushes of surprise;
From bulb and bush, from leaf and blade, spring up
Bell, disk, or star, plume, sceptre, fan, or cup;
A thousand forms, a thousand hues of bloom
Fill earth and heaven with beauty and perfume.
All this, by thine enchantment, liveth here;
Oh wondrous power, that chills my pride with fear!"

Pausias
"Thy praise, sweet critic, makes thee doubly dear.
But what of thy fair self, thy form, thy face,
The flower of flowers, the gracefulness of grace?"

Glycera
"I see why thou hast placed me among these;
I serve a purpose, 'tis to scare the bees.
Sweet love hath right to place me anywhere;
And yet I mourn, to find myself so fair."

Pausias
"A maid lament her beauty! Thou hast shown,
A thousand times, a wit beyond mine own;
Yet is it kind to such a love as mine,
To grudge it refuge in a lovely shrine?"

Glycera
"No shrine, no throne, of earth or heaven above,
Can be too fair a dwelling-place for love.
But that which makes me grieve, myself to see,
Is memory of the bitter loss to thee;
That earthly charms, as men such things esteem
Should tantalize thee, in a weeping dream!"

Pausias
"My own, my only love, what wouldst thou say?
My heart hath borne a heavy bode, all day."

Glycera
"I durst not tell thee, till thy work was done;
But now I must, before the setting sun.
Last night, when life was lapsed in quietude,
Beside my couch a stately figure stood
A virgin form, in garb of chace arrayed,

With bow and quiver, baldric, and steel blade;
Majestic as a palm that scorns the wind,
And taller than the daughters of mankind
Twas Artemis, close-girt in silver sheen,
The Goddess of the woods, the Maiden-queen.
Cold terror seized me, and mute awe, the while
She oped her proud lips, with an icy smile
'Whose votary art thou? Shall I resign
'To wanton Cypris this sworn nymph of mine?
'Have I enfeoffed thee of my holiest glen?
'To have thee tainted by the lips of men?
'Shall urchin Eros laugh at my decree?
'No Hymen torch, no loosened zone for thee I
'To-morrow, when my crescent tops yon oak,
'Thou shalt return unto thy proper yoke.'
She closed her lips, and like the barb of frost,
Her fingers on my bounding heart outspread:
My breast is ice, mv soul is of the dead:
The sod, the cold clay, are my marriage-bed;
Sweet sun, sweet flowers, sweet Love, forever lost!"

Pausias
"I'll not endure it; it shall ne'er be true;
If that cold tyrant comes, I'll run her through."

Glycera
"What can'st thou do against the Goddess trine,
Selene, Artemis, and Proserpine?
Oh love, thou hast before thee life and fame,
And some new Glycera with a loftier name.
So tender is my heart, that it would break,
To think that thou wert suffering for my sake.
Be angry with me; doubt my faith, or try;
And count it for a crime of mine to die:
Or tell thyself, if still a pain there be
That wealth and grandeur were not meant for me.
Yet think sometimes, when thou art well consoled,
That no one loves thee, like someone of old."

Pausias
"My life, my soul, my heart of hearts, my all,
Together let us cling, till death befall."

Glycera
"The sun is gone; the crescent waxeth bright;
I fly to darkness, or eternal light.
Great are the Gods; but greater yet is love;

Here thou art mine, and I am thine above."

Pausias
"Oh fame, and conquest, pomp, and power, and state,
What are ye, when the heart is desolate?
A few more years of labour, and slow breath
Till death benign hath overtaken death."

BUSCOMBE; OR, A MICHAELMAS GOOSE

When I was Head of Blunders school,
Before the age of stokers,
Compelled by rank to look a fool
Betwixt a pair of "chokers,"

Tom Tanner's father's wrote, to say
That we should both of us come,
To spend Saint Michael's holiday
At the Vicarage of Buscombe.

One trifle marred this merry plan
I had contrived, though barr'd up,
To typify the future man,
By getting very hard up.

Oh bimetallic champion, some
New ratio doth seem proper,
When the circulating medium
Has fallen to half a copper.

Vile mammon hence!   Thy low amount
Too paltry is to mope for;
The more we have in hand to count,
The less in heart to hope for.

Bright youth itself is golden ore,
And health the best gold-beater:
Without a sigh for two pence more,
We passed the gates of Peter.

A nod suffices surly Cop,
Who grins his bona fides;
As Cerberus preferred his sop
To Orpheus and Alcides.

But Mother Cop!   Her cooking knack
Would conquer fifty Catos

The Queen of tarts, and tuck, and tack,
And cream, and fried potatoes.

And rashers!   Sweet Ulysses, say
Old Homer was mistaken;
The Goddess must have had her way,
And turned thee into bacon.

That Circe came, and wished us joy,
And said, "Goodbye, my dearie!"
Because I was an honest boy,
And pauper tneo ære.

So Tom and I, like men on strike,
Shook hands with all our cronies,
Walked fifty yards, to save the pike,
And jumped upon our ponies.

Of apples, nuts, and goose galore
I chattered, like a stupid,
And thought of shooting coneys, more
Than being shot by Cupid.

At racing pace the turnpike road
(Great Western, in this quicker age)
Was swallowed up with whip and goad,
And soon we saw the Vicarage.

A sweet seclusion, to forget
The world and its disasters,
And fill the mind with mignonette,
Clove-pinks, and German asters;

In pensive, or in playful mood,
To saunter here, and dally
With leafy calm of solitude,
Or sunshine of the valley.

The Vicar loved his parish well,
And well was he loved by it;
Religion did not him compel
To harass and defy it

No price he charged for Heavenly love,
No discount on Resurgo;
His conscience told him, one side-shove
Is worth ten kicks a tergo.

But while the path of life he showed
To win the Christian guerdon,
No post was he, to point the road,
But a man to share the burden.

The lapse of years made manifest
The sanctuary of holy age;
As clearer grows the ring-dove's nest,
When time hath stripp'd the foliage.

The Vicar's wife was much the same,
In fairer form presented
A lively, yet a quiet dame,
With home, sweet home, contented.

In parish, needs; and household arts,
A lesson to this glib age;
Well versed in pickles, jams, and tarts,
Piano, chess, and cribbage.

And well she loved the flowers, that speak
A language undefiled
The flowers that lift the dimpled cheek,
Or droop the dewy eyelid.

Now, if she lingers after us,
What ground have we for snarling?
What act prohibits private buss,
Reserved for "Tommy darling"?

But who are these, so fresh and sweet,
In lovely hats and dresses,
Who half advance, and half retreat,
And peep through clouds of tresses?

"Come, dears!" They shyly offer hand,
Beneath the jasmin trellis;
"Say who you are, girls" Charlotte, and
Her sister, Caroline Ellis!

Sweet Charlotte hath a serious face,
A gaze almost parental;
A type of every maiden grace,
But a wee bit sentimental.

Bright Caroline hath eyes that dance,

While buoyant airs engirdle her;
Her playful soul may love romance,
But not a creepy curdler.

Sweet Charlotte's are the deep grey eyes
That win profound devotion;
Bright Carry's flash, like azure skies,
With heliograph in motion.

As merry as the vintage ray,
That dances down the grape-rill;
As tender as the dews of May,
Or apple-buds of April.

Their charms are safe to grow more bright
For at least two lustral stages;
And so it seems not unpolite
To enquire what their age is.

"Last May, I was fifteen"; with glee
Replies the laughing Carry;
Sage Charlotte adds "And I shall be
Seventeen, next February."

To the dining-room we walk on air,
Disdaining jots and tittles;
To feed seems such a low affair
And yet, hurrah for victuals!

Could e'en a boy ply knife and fork,
In presence so poetic,
Until the vicar draws a cork,
And gives the sniff prophetic?

And when the evening games began,
Pope Joan, and Speculation
What head could keep its poise and plan,
With the heart in palpitation?

Until, in soft white-curtained bed,
We sink to slumber lowly,
And angels fan the childish head,
With visions sweet and holy.

"Now I do declare," exclaimed our host,
As he strode back from the arish,
"Those railway fellows soon will boast

They have undermined my parish!

"Though none can say I have ever set
My face against improvement,
I cannot quite perceive as yet
The good of this new movement

"Like Hannibal, these folk confound
All nature's institutions,
And shun, with a great dive underground,
Parochial contributions!

"Come boys and girls, let us see their craft,
These hills of Devon will task it;
'Tis a pretty walk to White-Ball shaft,
If the boys will take a basket

"Dear wife; if your poor feet are right,
The miracles of this cycle
Will give you a noble appetite,
For the roast goose of Saint Michael."

In a twinkle, we had baskets twain
Of the right stuff for a journey,
And beautiful gooseberry Champagne,
Superior to Epernay,

What myriad joys of heart and mind
Flit in and out our brief age!
That day it was grand to see how kind
The sun looked through the leafage!

While the leaves for their part pricked their lips,
With a dewy simper waiting;
They were conscious of some amber tips
But those Were his own creating.

Can the heart of man alone be dull,
And the mind of man be spiteful,
When all above is beautiful,
And all below delightful?

When Season bright, and Season rich,
Make bids against each other;
And earth, uncertain which is which,
Smiles up at Nature Mother.

The copse, the lane, the meadow path,
The valleys, banks, and hedges,
Were green with summer's aftermath,
And gold with autumn's pledges.

Wild rose hung coral beads above,
And satchel'd nuts grew nigh them;
Like tips of a little maiden's glove,
Ere ever she has to buy them.

But ours are not the maids to bite
A gore or gusset undone;
How neat they look, how trim and tight!
Those frocks were made in London.

Long time, we glance in awe and doubt,
Suppressing all frivolity;
Till the spirit of the age breaks out,
And all is mirth and jollity.

One flash, that stole from eyes demure,
Hath scattered all convention;
And then a pearly laugh makes sure
That fun is her intention.

The smiling elders march ahead;
We dance, without a fiddler,
We play at cross-touch, White and Red,
Tip-cat, and Tommy Tidier.

We laugh and shout, much more than speak,
No etiquette importunes;
The trees were made for hide-and-seek,
The flowers to tell our fortunes;

The hills, for pretty girls to pant,
And glow with richer roses;
The wind itself, to toss askant
The curls that hide their noses.

Then sprightly Carry shouts in French
"All boys and girls, come nutting!"
We are slipping down a mighty trench
Why, it is the Railway cutting I

Before us yawns a dark-browed arch,
Paved with a muddy runnel;

A thousand giant navvies march
To delve the White-Ball tunnel.

Oh, if a man of them but did
Presume to glance at Carry,
Though he were Milo, or John Ridd,
I would toss him to Old Harry.

I pull my jacket off, like him
Who would shatter England's pillars
From the tunnel comes an order grim,
"Get out of the way you chillers!"

And the same stern order doth apply
To the pranks of this remote age!
We are sure alike to be thrust by,
In our nonage, and our dotage.

Yet who shall grudge the tranquil age,
When nought can now betide ill,
To glance, from a distant hermitage,
At a summer morning idyll?

Oh agony, despair, and woe!
Oh two-edged sword to us come!
To Blundell's must the body go,
While the heart remains at Buscombe.

All breakfast time, how glum we looked!
Our tears were threatening dribblets;
Too truly had our goose been cooked,
To leave us e'en our giblets.

Sweet Charlotte, did you share the thrill,
The pang; no throat may utter,
And strive an aching void to fill
With heartless toast and butter?

And were you sad, bright Caroline,
Although you never said so?
You did cast down your lovely eyne,
And you crumbled up your bread so!

But the Vicar's views were more sublime,
As he asked in all simplicity,
"My youthful friends, what is the prime
Of all mundane felicity?"

My answer, though it sounded cool,
Was given with trepidation
"To stay at home, and send to school
The rising generation."

A gentle smile flits o'er his lip,
He eyes me with benignity;
He yearns to offer goodly tip,
Yet fears to wound my dignity.

True benefactor, be not shy,
Thou seest a humble fellow,
Thy noble impulse gratify.
My stars, if it isn't yellow!

But time is over, and above,
To end this charming visit;
And must we part my own true love?
Though I am not sure, which is it.

Sweet Charlotte lingered in the shade,
Most gentle of all houris;
Bright Carry in the lobby played
With a pair of polished cowries.

She showed me how alike they were,
So Heaven had pleased to make them.
Though fortune might divide the pair,
She ne'er could separate them.

I blushed, and stammered at her touch,
I feared to beg for either;
My heart was in my mouth so much,
I could say "Goodbye" to neither.

Two strings are wise for every bow,
To meet the change of weather;
And Cupid's shafts give softer blow,
When two are tied together.

Oh, Charlotte sweet, and Carry bright,
My whole, or double-half love,
Let no maturer wisdom slight
A simple tale of calf-love.

A blessing on the maiden grace,

That beautifies the real,
To make the world a fairer place,
And lift the low ideal!

If one, or both, by any chance,
Behold what I confess here,
Make auld lang syne of young romance,
By sending your address here.

And answer, as I trust you can,
When time is flying faster,
That he hath served you better than
Your humble poetaster.

Postscript (a Fact)
This have they done, and oh, by Jove,
Not altered by a fraction!
If then they were too sweet to love,
What are they now? Distraction.

Of course they must be ever young;
How could I be so stupid?
Time fell in love with both, and flung
His calendar to Cupid!

TO FAME

I
Right Fairy of the morn, with flowers arrayed,
Whose beauties to thy young pursuer seem
Beyond the ecstasy of poet's dream
Shall I overtake thee, ere thy lustre fade?

II
Ripe glory of the noon, august, and proud,
A vision of high purpose, power, and skill,
That melteth into mirage of good-will
Do I o'ertake thee, or embrace a cloud?

III
Gray shadow of the evening, gaunt and bare,
At random cast, beyond me or above,
And cold as memory in the arms of love
If I o'ertook thee now, what should I care?

IV

"No morn, or noon, or eve am I," she said;

"But night, the depth of night behind the sun;
By all mankind pursued; but never won,
Until my shadow falls upon a shade."

1894.

www.ingramcontent.com/pod-product-compliance
Lightning Source LLC
Chambersburg PA
CBHW071346130626
46556CB00005B/2060